BLUEWATER JOURNAL

The Voyage of the SEA TIGER

LORETTA KRUPINSKI

HarperCollins*Publishers*

PACIFIC OCEAN

NORTH AMERICA

ATLANTIC OCEAN

BOSTON

SANDWICH
ISLANDS

EQUATOR

SOUTH AMERICA

RIO JANEIRO

VOYAGE
OF THE
CLIPPER SHIP
Sea Tiger

CAPE HORN

AUTHOR'S NOTE

Bluewater Journal is inspired by authentic logbooks, journals, and letters found at the Mystic Seaport Museum in Mystic, Connecticut. This story is told from the point of view of a boy who keeps a journal as his family travels around the Americas. Their ship sails from Boston in April 1860, rounds Cape Horn, and arrives in Hawaii, known then as the Sandwich Islands, four months later. They travel by the fastest mode of transportation available at the time: a clipper ship called *Sea Tiger*, 180 feet long and 36 feet wide.

I wish to thank the staff at the Mystic Seaport Museum for their time and help on this project.

This book is dedicated to those who have a romance with the sea and its ships.

—Loretta Krupinski

April 8, 1860

"I christen you the *Sea Tiger*; may you ever sail swiftly and safely to your ports." The big clipper ship then slid into Boston Harbor. When the cargo of six cases of copper, 200 boxes of soap, 250 barrels of flour, 100 kegs of nails, one piano, and assorted boxes of nails and tools was finally stored below, I, Benjamin Slocum, began my voyage. Together with my father, who is the ship's captain, my mother, and my sister, Isabel, we are bound for Cape Horn and Honolulu.

I am sad to think that I will not see my friends and grandparents for a long time. However, the feeling of Christmas hung over our departure, for we received so many presents. Our cook, Ah Ling, gave my mother a jar of ginger; Grandma gave us preserves; Grandpa gave me a journal so I could write about my voyage; and Uncle Samuel presented me with a fine box of watercolors and several sketchbooks. We set sail from Boston Harbor with a fair wind and soon passed Boston Light. When I am grown up, I want to have a ship like this of my own.

April 10, 1860

Mother and Isabel have been seasick. I have been taking care of them, as Papa is busy up on deck. In the main stateroom are a new carpet and Papa's easy chair. Mama's house plants make it almost seem like home. Our beds swing down from chains so we roll with the ship. My room is on the port side. When I am in my bed, I can hear the water splashing by on the side near my head. Our food comes packed in barrels, and the cook makes good cornbread served with molasses.

I do not like it very much when we have stormy weather. Mama, Isabel, and I have to stay below, and it is dark and dreary there. Sometimes we all get seasick again. Mama is knitting sweaters for Isabel and me, as Papa says it will be very cold when we round Cape Horn. When it is summer in Boston, it will be winter down there. Isabel plays with her dolls and stitches a sampler. We also play lotto and card games. I have won almost all the time, but not at chess. Papa always wins. When I want to be alone, I write in my journal, read a book, or paint in my sketchbook. I tack up my best paintings in my cabin. Mama wants us to be smart when we grow up, so she teaches us spelling, reading, and arithmetic. I want to be smart so I can be a great sea captain like Papa.

April 25, 1860

One of my chores is to take care of the animals we have brought on board. We have Nanny the goat for milk, several pigs for fresh pork, a few chickens, and a handsome but mean rooster. The cook sends Isabel and me to gather eggs from the chickens. When we get close to them, the rooster strikes out at us. We have to drop the eggs so we can protect ourselves. Sometimes the rooster rides on top of Nanny's back, and Nanny tries to throw him off. It makes us all laugh. Later I will make a painting of a pig.

I stay on deck as much as I can and watch the crew work. Sometimes I'm allowed to help. I also keep a lookout for another ship. The ship is called *Morning Star*, and we are in a race with her. The captain of the ship that reaches Honolulu first will win a new telescope. I am already worried that we will lose, as *Morning Star* sailed two days earlier from Boston.

April 30, 1860

We have crossed the Equator and endured a powerful storm. Lightning struck one of our masts, but the rain poured down so hard it kept the ship from catching on fire. The waves rolled us about with a thunderous booming sound. Every timber inside the ship creaked. Added to this was the clatter from the galley as pots, kettles, and plates flew through the air. The sea pushed open the hatchway doors, and we took out twenty buckets of water. There was no rest anywhere for anyone. It was my first big storm at sea and it was so exciting that I only felt a tiny bit afraid.

The rain has filled our water casks. Mama is happy, for now she can do her washing and we can all have baths.

The days grow shorter. The sun is only a few degrees above the horizon. There are no more gales, but the crew let out the sails only to take them back in because of the changing winds.

I still have not seen the sails of the *Morning Star*. I worry we will not win the race.

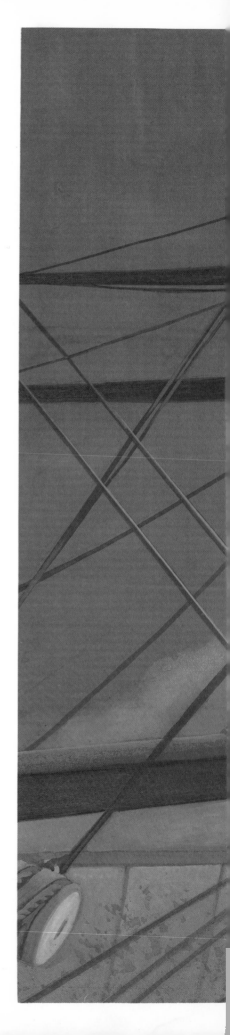

May 8, 1860

We have sailed thirty days and have arrived at the port of Rio Janeiro in Brazil. My legs still feel as if the land is rolling up and down. We will be here a week to off-load our cargo because there is more work than men to do it. The *Morning Star* will really have a big lead on us now.

We were relieved to travel from the crowded, dirty city and go to where the steep mountains meet the forests. We visited some people Mama and Papa know who used to live in Boston. Their children let us play with their pet monkey. Isabel and I wanted to take a monkey back to the ship with us, but Papa wouldn't allow it.

Today we all enjoyed a picnic at the Botanical Gardens. My nose is tired from sniffing so many flowers. From the garden we could look out over the harbor and see Sugarloaf, a very steep mountain.

We have been writing letters all week to our friends and relatives. Before we set sail, we will leave the letters ashore to be mailed to Boston. I am sending some small paintings to Uncle Samuel.

June 8, 1860

The carpenter, Mr. Adams, and Manuel, one of the crew, are my special friends. Mr. Adams helps me with my paintings and I help him with his work. Manuel is teaching me how to tie knots and I am teaching him English. He told me, "You don't use ropes on a ship, you use line, and you don't haul in a sail with a line, it's called a sheet." I am trying to learn enough to sail my own ship, but there is much to know and it is hard to remember it all.

Manuel made a ship model of the *Sea Tiger* for me. We will rig it together so I can learn the names of the lines.

During the dogwatch in early evening, and only during good weather or flat calms, the crew will light their pipes. Lying on our beds below, Isabel and I fall fast asleep while they sing seafaring folk songs called shanties.

June 15, 1860

When I am not busy, sometimes I like to watch the water for sea life. I have done some nice paintings of dolphins, sea turtles, and whales. Once when I wasn't looking and much to the surprise of everyone, a whale came so close to our ship as to spray our deck with his waterspout. Then he thrashed the sea with his flukes and went underwater.

Today we finally spied *Morning Star* and she is ahead of us. Father had the crew trim the sails and gave new orders to the helmsman. He was so excited that he offered an extra dollar to each of the crew if we win the race. Me too!

We also passed another ship heading north. Through our telescope we could see children waving back at us. On a chalkboard my father wrote our home port, where we're bound, and how many days we're out. They could read it with their telescope. They were from San Francisco, bound for New Bedford, and 82 days out.

June 30, 1860

We began rounding Cape Horn three days ago with much concern. It is here where the head winds and waters of two great oceans, the Atlantic and the Pacific, come together. The seas and winds are never at peace. The sun is often hidden by mists, clouds, and fog. Isabel says she is scared because it looks so gloomy. Passing near the shore, the mountains are rough and jagged, covered with snow. We could make out penguins with our telescope, even though it doesn't work so well. I hope Papa wins the new one.

The wind has moved the water to mountainous heights. An albatross followed in our wake with not another living thing in sight. The silence was broken only by the wind whistling through the rigging, sounding like a hornpipe playing a wild tune. It is cold below deck too. We snuggle under our quilts during the day, wearing the new sweaters that Mama made.

Morning Star is still ahead of us. The waves are so high we can only catch a glimpse of her.

July 7, 1860

We have rounded Cape Horn in ten days and have picked up head winds that will take us to the Sandwich Islands and Honolulu. To celebrate, the cook has killed a pig and we dined on roast pork with plum pudding duff for dessert. "Eat and drink your fill, and don't look forlorn. There's roasted pork and good-bye Cape Horn," said the cook.

I am glad to be allowed to go up on deck again. I'm even happy to try sneaking past the rooster to gather eggs.

We no longer see *Morning Star*. Father is worried that she might have been wrecked. I spent most of the morning looking for her.

August 12, 1860

"Land off the port bow," the mate cried out from above. Looking out, I could see the peaks of the mountains of the Sandwich Islands. At last! Papa says the mountains are different from the ones we have at home. They blow their tops, and hot liquid rock called lava runs down the side like molasses. The golden setting sun made them glow. Sounds of crashing surf were all around us as we passed a reef. A strong breeze took us through a channel between two of the islands. A pilot boat arrived and the pilot guided us into the crowded harbor. Upon the order "Let go!" the anchor dropped with a rumble and shook the ship from stem to stern.

Among the other ships and small craft, we are peacefully anchored under hundreds of stars. It is late and I am tired.

August 13, 1860

We were all up early today because the harbor is a noisy, busy place. Schooners, whalers, and clipper ships are all crowded together, making it difficult to see Honolulu through so much rigging.

In all the excitement yesterday, we forgot to look for *Morning Star*. Last night, I awoke and ran up on the deck to look for her. It was too dark to be sure she was there.

The island is fringed with trees, called palms, that look like green feathers. A tall mountain called Diamond Head is at one end. Little white cottages line the waterfront. In the harbor, people paddle canoes that have an outrigger attached to one side.

The American Consul has brought business papers for Papa to sign, letters from home, and an orchid for Mama.

I like not having the ship move. The air smells of earth and flowers. Isabel and I look down on the underwater forests and the beautifully colored fish. I am restless not being able to go ashore until tomorrow.

August 14, 1860

Morning Star, for lack of a strong wind, arrived last evening. We have won, and I get a dollar!

Today we were towed to a wharf. From the ship, we gazed down on people from all parts of the world and on the Kanakas, the name for the native people. Straw hats were twined with flowers, and garlands of flowers were worn around everyone's neck. I felt silly, but the Minister who greeted us gave us each our own garland.

We walked to the Hotel, which is our residence while we are here. A carriage took all of us to Palikea Mountain to see the volcano crater. Below us lay sugarcane fields and small farmhouses. The edge of the island was ringed with white surf.

Afterward, Isabel, Mama, and I went to the market. I spent my dollar on a horn that was made from a large seashell and on some coconut candy. We saw strange flowers and fruits. Imagine calling a fruit "breadfruit" when it doesn't look or taste anything like bread.

August 29, 1860

We were in Honolulu for fifteen days, loading a new cargo to take to Hong Kong. We also loaded new supplies for ourselves, including new chickens, a friendlier rooster, and Papa's new telescope. On a rising tide and strong wind, we left in the afternoon.

I think how much I like to see the canvas stretch in a gale, and listen to the masts creaking and the wind piping through the rigging. Leaning on the rail, I grew drowsy and came below to write this in my journal. Soon I will be fast asleep, not even bothering to listen to the water rushing by on the side near my head.

AFTERWORD

Clipper ships were built for speed and for carrying cargo and passengers. After the California gold discovery in 1848, clipper ships sailed to San Francisco from New York or Boston and then on to the silk and tea markets in China and India. More than two hundred clippers were built in shipyards along the coast from Maine to New York. For twenty years the "Greyhounds of the Sea" crisscrossed paths around the world until the American Civil War started and steam-powered vessels came into common use.

A clipper ship is the only vessel to carry square sails on its three masts. One of the fastest clippers was the *Flying Cloud*, built 229 feet long and 40 feet wide. In a record-breaking voyage, she sailed from New York to San Francisco in 89 days.

Long ocean voyages caused much stress and damage to the ships. Most of them were eventually burned, wrecked, or abandoned. Today, only one clipper ship still survives: the *Cutty Sark*, now berthed in Greenwich, England.

GLOSSARY

EQUATOR: the imaginary line around the Earth, midway between the North and South poles

DOGWATCH: a lookout or watch on the deck from 4-6 P.M. or 6-8 P.M.

GALLEY: the place on a vessel where the cooking is done

HATCHWAY: an opening in the deck; a passageway to go above and below deck

MAST: a round timber set upright from the deck to support the rigging

PILOT BOAT: a small vessel used to drop off a pilot who then guides an incoming vessel into a harbor

PORT: the left side of a vessel as you look forward

SHEET: a rope used to take in or set a sail

STEM: a nearly upright timber that runs lengthwise and becomes the forward member of a vessel's hull

STERN: the rear end of a vessel

YARD: a tapered round piece of wood to which a square sail is fastened. It is hung at its center to a mast. It is raised or lowered to set or take in a sail.

S E A   T I G E R

180 feet length overall, 36 feet wide, 1860, Boston, Massachusetts

The full-page illustrations in this book were painted with gouache and colored pencil on sabretooth paper and the spot illustrations were painted with watercolors on Strathmore 500 watercolor paper.

Colwell Handletter, the typeface used in this book, was designed by Elizabeth Colwell, the first American woman type designer, in 1917.

Bluewater Journal
The Voyage of the SEA TIGER
Copyright © 1995 by Loretta Krupinski

Library of Congress Cataloging-in-Publication Data
Krupinski, Loretta.
    Bluewater journal : the voyage of the Sea Tiger / Loretta Krupinski.
       p.   cm.
    Summary: Twelve-year-old Benjamin Slocum keeps his own journal as he travels with his family from Boston to Honolulu in the clipper ship Sea Tiger.
    ISBN 0-06-023436-9. — ISBN 0-06-023437-7 (lib. bdg.)
    [1. Clipper ships—Fiction.   2. Diaries—Fiction.] I. Title.
PZ7.K94624B1 1995   94-13241
[E]—dc20   CIP
                                                    AC

Typography by Christine Kettner
1 2 3 4 5 6 7 8 9 10
❖
First Edition